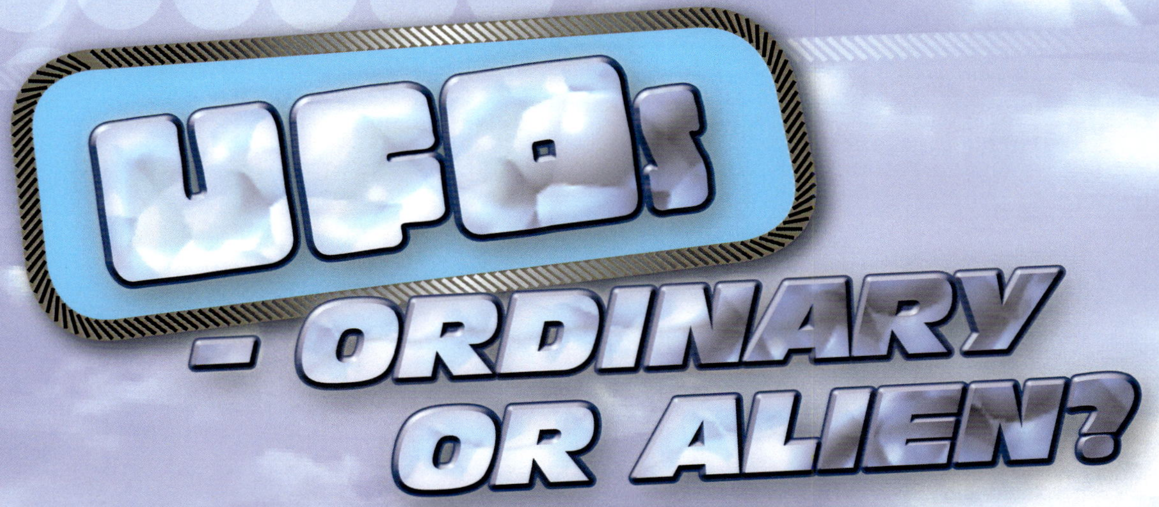

Australia • Brazil • Japan • Korea • Mexico • Singapore • Spain • United Kingdom • United States

UFOs – Ordinary or Alien?

Fast Forward
Orange Level 15

Text: Carmel Reilly
Editor: Cameron Macintosh
Design: Stella Vassiliou
Series design: James Lowe
Production controller: Emma Hayes
Photo research: Gillian Cardinal
Audio recordings: Juliet Hill, Picture Start
Spoken by: Matthew King and Abbe Holmes
Reprint: Jennifer Foo

Acknowledgements
The author and publisher would like to acknowledge permission to reproduce material from the following sources: Photographs by Alamy/Stephen Saks Photography, p 10 bottom; APL/Corbis/Bettman, p 22; Mary Evans Picture Library, pp 10-11, 16, 23; Photolibrary.com/Imagestate Ltd, front cover, pp 1, 3, 6/ Science Photo Library, pp 5, 7, 8, 9 top & bottom, 12, 14, 15, 17/ Image source, p 18/ Graham Monro, pp 20-21.

ISBN 978 0 17 012607 6
ISBN 978 0 17 012597 0 (set)

Cengage Learning Australia
Level 7, 80 Dorcas Street
South Melbourne, Victoria Australia 3205
Phone: 1300 790 853

Cengage Learning New Zealand
Unit 4B Rosedale Office Park
331 Rosedale Road, Albany, North Shore NZ 0632
Phone: 0508 635 766

For learning solutions, visit cengage.com.au

Printed in Australia by Ligare Pty Ltd
7 8 9 10 11 12 13 21 20 19 18 17

Evaluated in independent research by staff from the Department of Language, Literacy and Arts Education at the University of Melbourne.

UFOs – Ordinary or Alien?

Carmel Reilly

Contents

Chapter 1

ABOUT UFOs

UFOs – **Unidentified** Flying Objects – are not new. There have been UFO sightings in our skies for thousands of years.

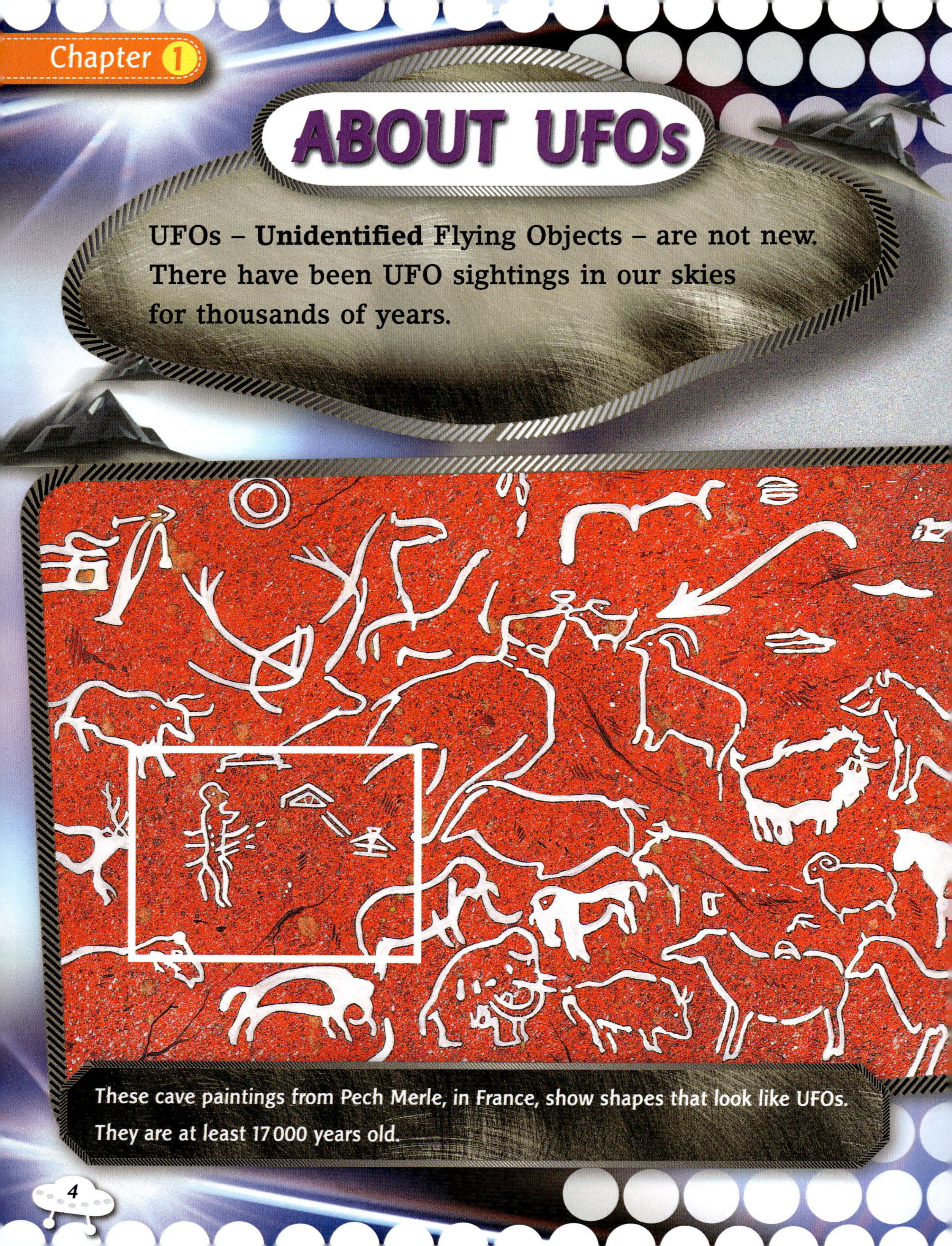

These cave paintings from Pech Merle, in France, show shapes that look like UFOs. They are at least 17 000 years old.

UFOs have been seen in many forms, from fast-moving lights to 'flying saucers'. As yet, no one knows what UFOs really are, but many people have very strong ideas about them.

There are two main ideas about UFOs.
One idea is that UFOs are alien space ships
from across the universe,
which have come to check on us and our planet.

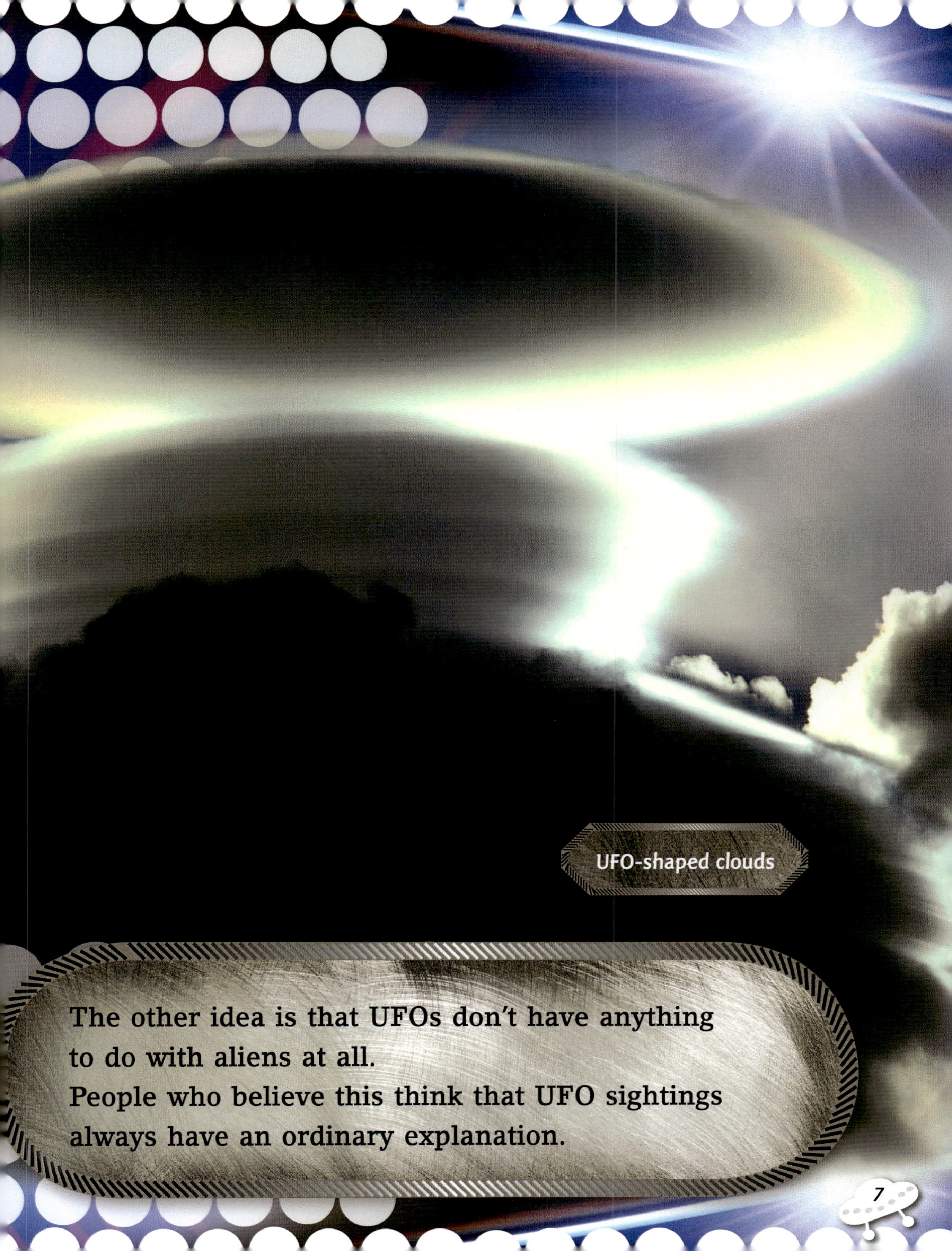

The other idea is that UFOs don't have anything to do with aliens at all.
People who believe this think that UFO sightings always have an ordinary explanation.

UNEXPLAINED SIGHTINGS

There are hundreds and hundreds of UFO sightings every year. Almost all of them can be explained as something ordinary.

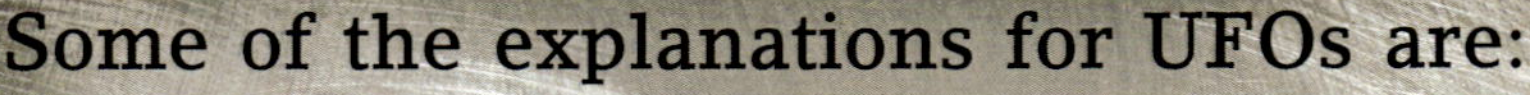

Some of the explanations for UFOs are:

- lights from Earth
- stars, planets or **meteors**
- planes and other spacecraft from Earth
- strange-shaped clouds
- hoaxes (people playing tricks).

Running Words 154

But, no matter how hard some people have tried, there have always been a few sightings that cannot be explained.

UFO-shaped clouds

Some unexplained sightings are:

- Roswell, New Mexico, USA, 1947
- Rendelsham Forest, England, 1980
- Nullarbor Plain, Australia, 1988
- Mexico City, Mexico, 1991.

Roswell, New Mexico

flat trees in Rendelsham Forest, England

In some places, there have been signs of UFO crashes such as marks on the ground and bits of rubbish that cannot be explained.

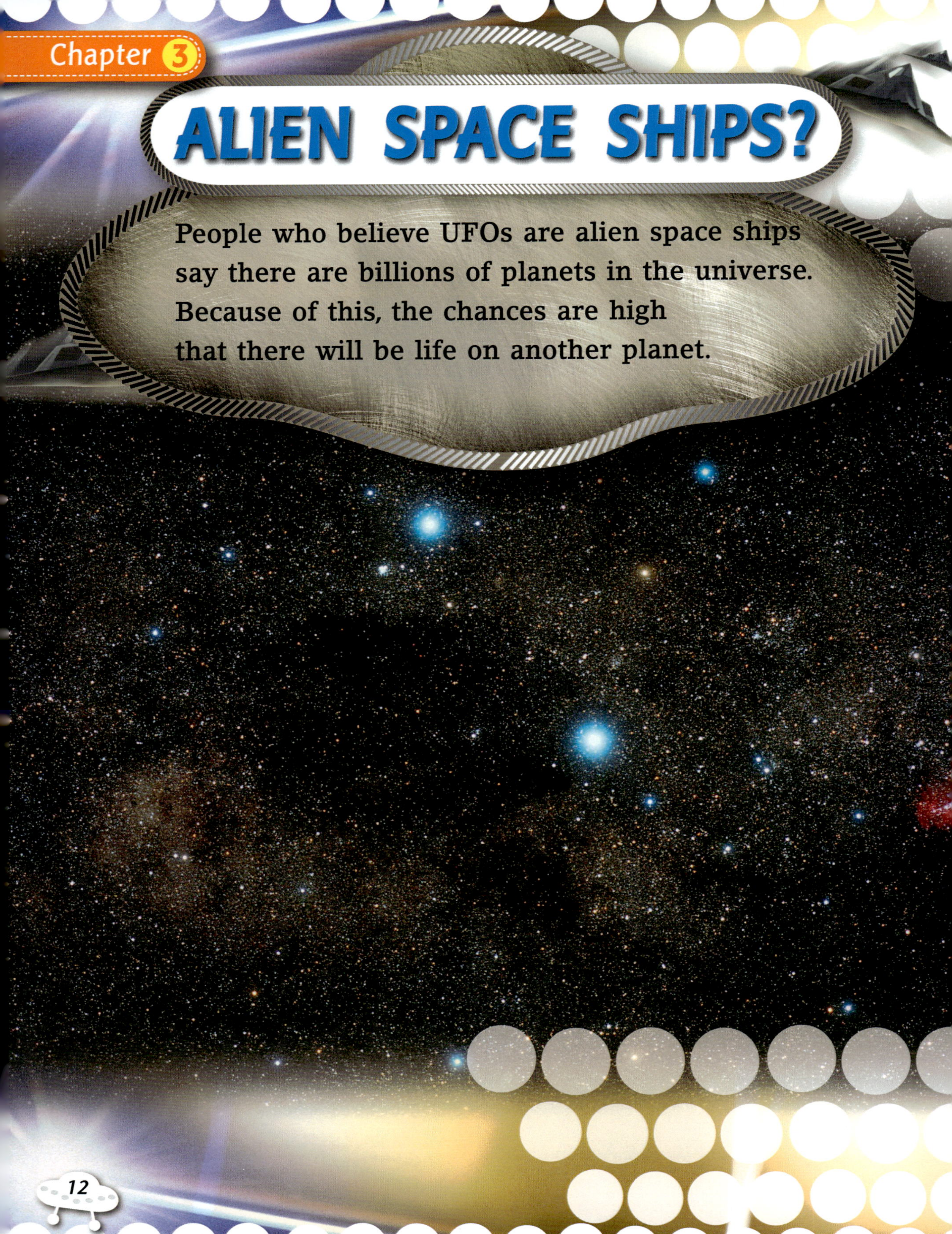

Chapter 3

ALIEN SPACE SHIPS?

People who believe UFOs are alien space ships say there are billions of planets in the universe. Because of this, the chances are high that there will be life on another planet.

These believers say it is very likely that UFOs could be visitors from other planets.

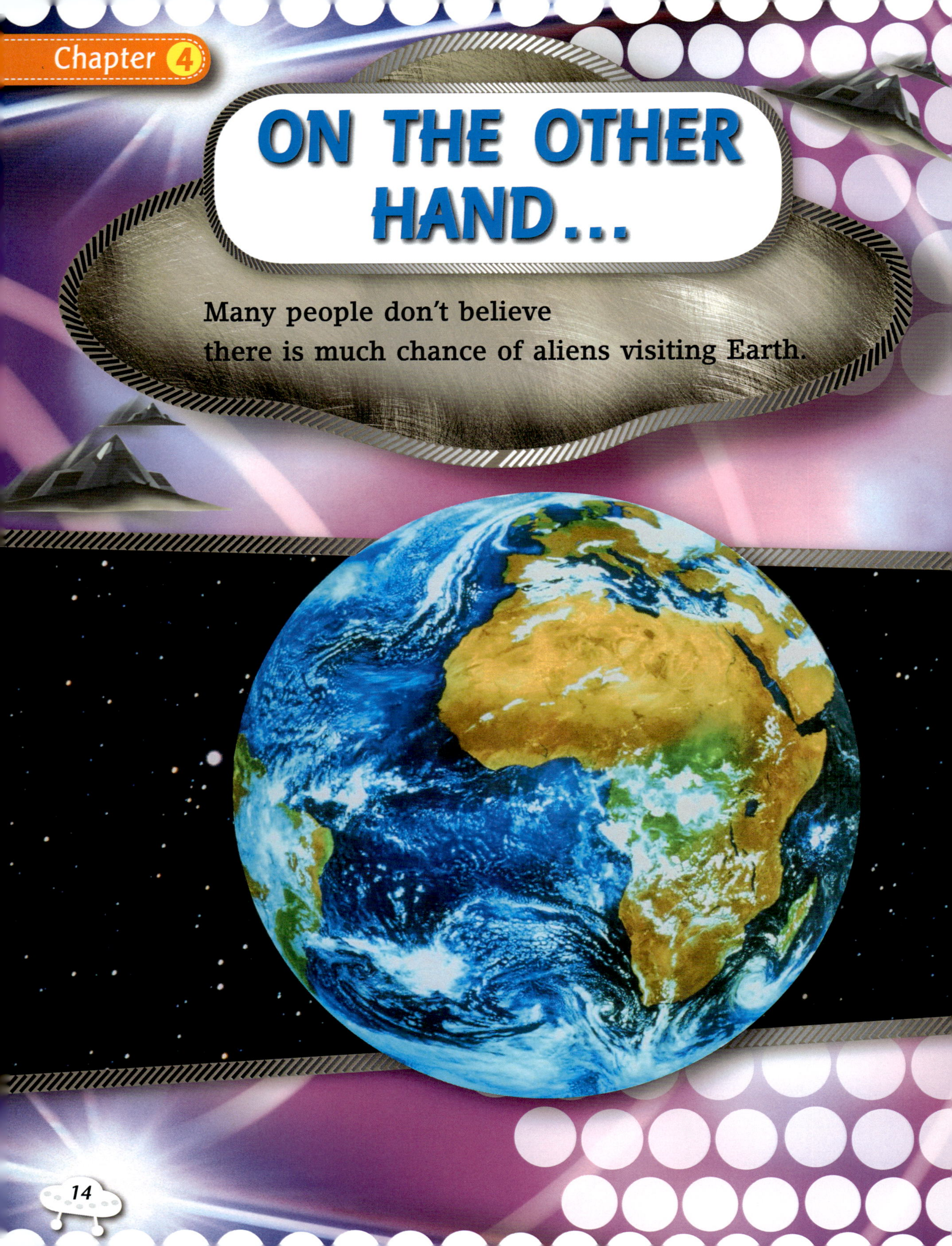

Chapter 4

ON THE OTHER HAND...

Many people don't believe
there is much chance of aliens visiting Earth.

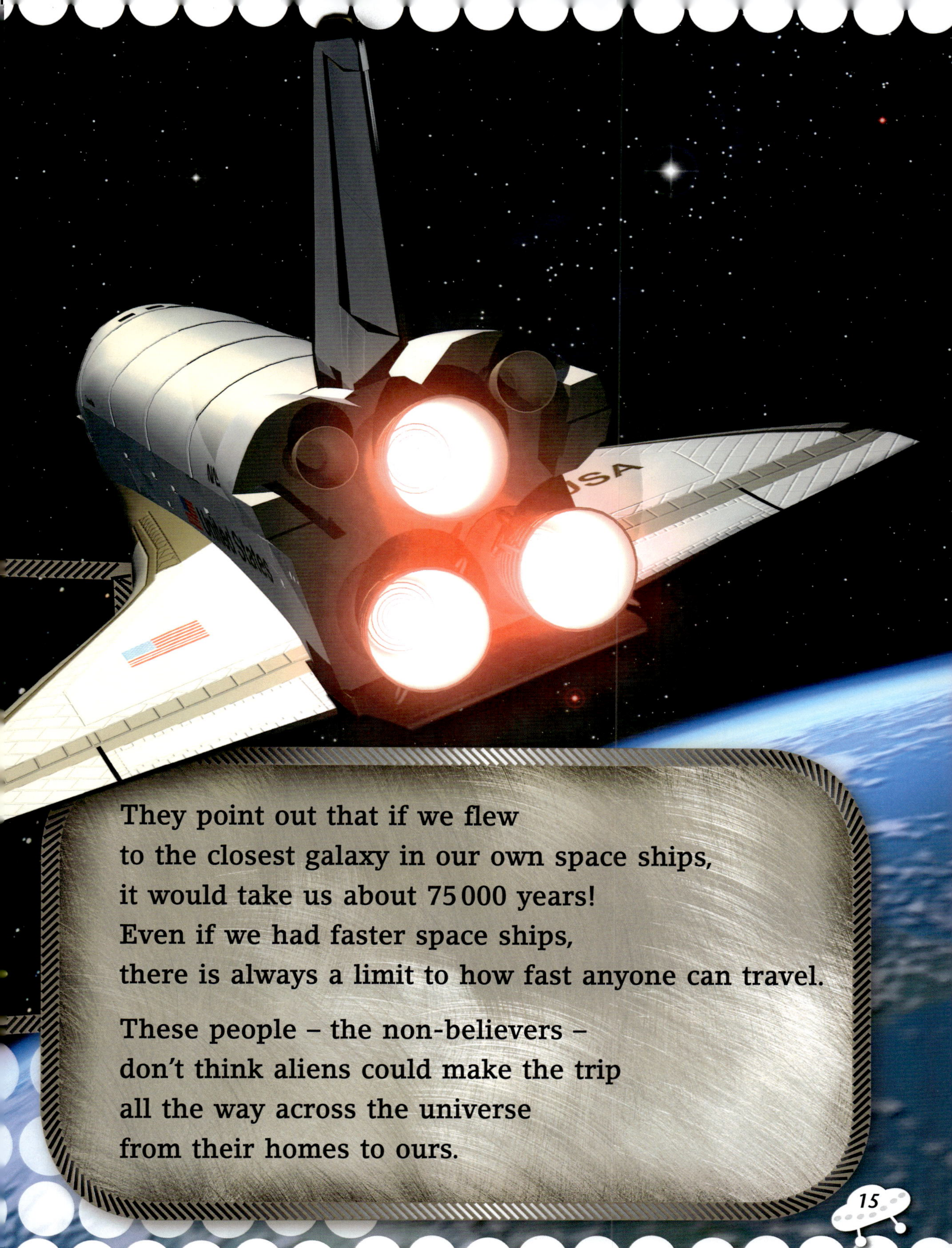

They point out that if we flew
to the closest galaxy in our own space ships,
it would take us about 75 000 years!
Even if we had faster space ships,
there is always a limit to how fast anyone can travel.

These people – the non-believers –
don't think aliens could make the trip
all the way across the universe
from their homes to ours.

Chapter 5

PROOF

As well as sightings, there are a lot of photos and even some films of UFOs. Believers say that these are proof that aliens are visiting Earth.

But non-believers say no.

A lot of photos have been found to be fake, and many photos are not very clear – or could be other things.

The non-believers say there is no hard proof that UFOs are alien space ships.

They ask why no one has ever been able to get hold of any alien clothing,
or parts of their space ships.

On the other hand, there have been many UFO sightings over the years. A lot of these sightings have been made by aircraft pilots who know the skies well.

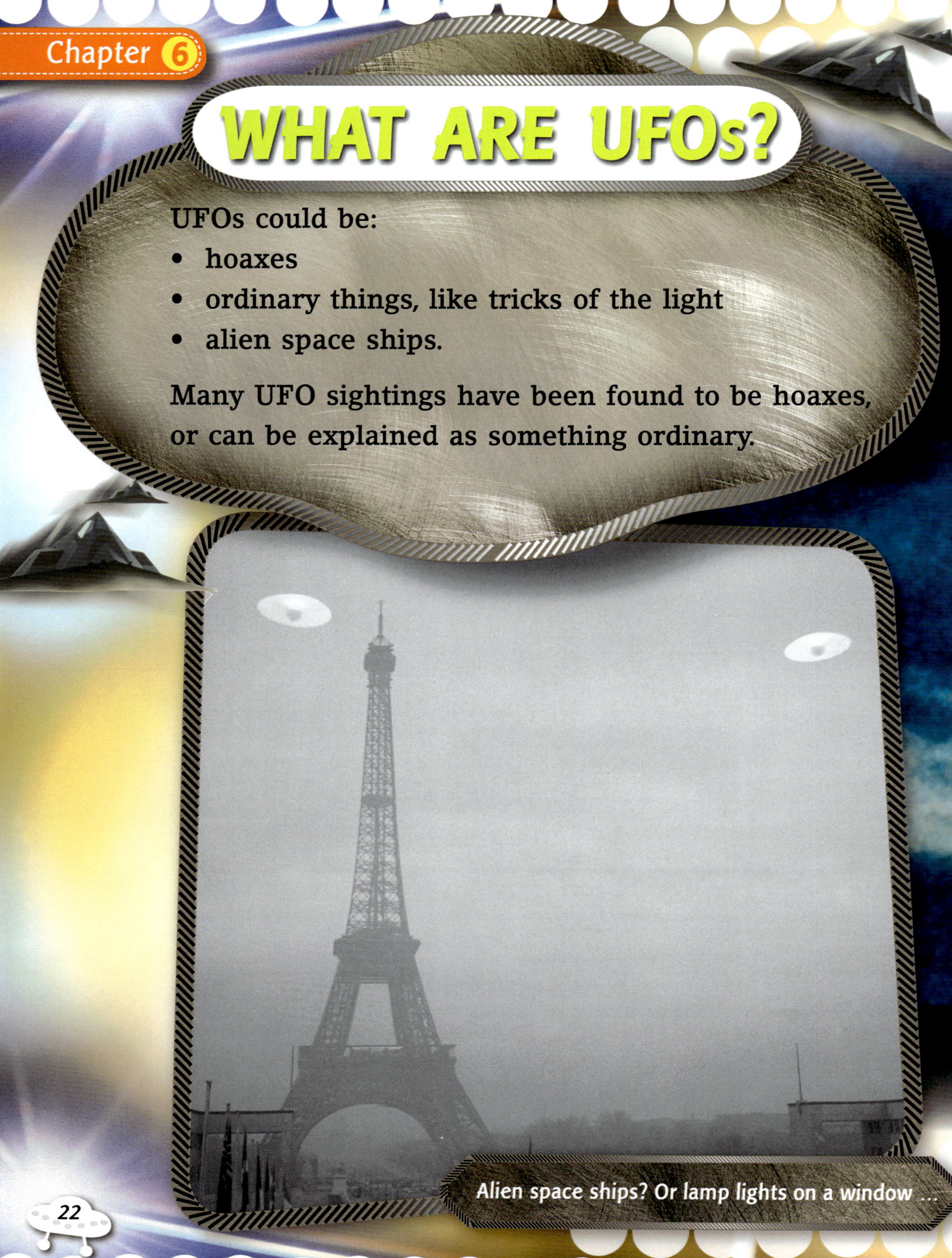

Chapter 6

WHAT ARE UFOs?

UFOs could be:

- hoaxes
- ordinary things, like tricks of the light
- alien space ships.

Many UFO sightings have been found to be hoaxes, or can be explained as something ordinary.

Alien space ships? Or lamp lights on a window …

However, every year, there are always some sightings that cannot be explained in any of those ways.

Glossary

meteor a rock or other object that comes to Earth from space

unidentified something is said to be unidentified when nobody knows what it is

Index